Chapter One

Ever since Ratso dropped into my back garden in his damaged spaceship my life has not been the same. Mum and Dad believe Ratso is just a pet rat – Mum thinks he's cute and Dad thinks he's a waste of space – but to me he's a big responsibility. I mean, how do you look after something that everyone thinks is a pet when really it's a creature from another planet?

A creature, let me tell you, with a mind of its own.

One day, not long after he arrived, Ratso and I were having an argument.

"Gosh-durn it, pardner!" he said in his favourite cowboy accent. "Now why in tarnation can't I go to your school? I *am* a teacher on my own planet, you know." The little alien glowered. "Perhaps you think your teacher won't match up to me?"

I stared at the bristling little creature with its fuzz-top hairstyle, pink eyes and twitching tail for a few seconds then burst out laughing.

My Rat is a Teacher

FRANK RODGERS

MACDONALD YOUNG BOOKS

Text and illustrations copyright © Frank Rodgers 1999

First published in Great Britain in 1999
by Macdonald Young Books
an imprint of Wayland Publishers Ltd
61 Western Road
Hove
East Sussex
BN3 1JD

Find Macdonald Young Books on the internet at
http://www.myb.co.uk

Designed by Don Martin
Printed and bound by Guernsey Press

British Library Cataloguing in Publication Data available

ISBN: 0 7500 2823 8

J111,590
£8.50

"What's so doggone funny?" Ratso spluttered, hopping about angrily on the edge of my chest of drawers beside his cage.

"You," I said, grinning. "You talk as if you can just walk into my class and have a chat with Mr Anderton."

"Of course I could!" snapped Ratso. "I'm going to try and speak your language to him. I'm sure he'll understand me." He smirked.

"Teachers are smart. He won't need the ear-piece translator that I had to give you. Me and your Mr Anderton could have a mighty fine discussion about timetabling, curriculum, exams and homework."

"No you couldn't!" I yelped. "There's no way you could do that! Andy Pandy would have a fit! Can you imagine? He'd want to know how a pet rat—"

"I am *not* a pet, gosh-durn it!"

"All right. I mean how a *talking* rat came to be in his classroom. And when he found out you're an alien – a *Wheesh* from the planet *Whee* – then your feet wouldn't touch the ground. He'd have you whisked out of school and into the nearest government research laboratory before you could say 'Boo'!"

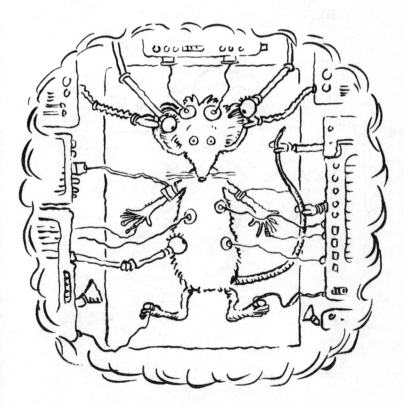

"Why in tarnation would I want to say 'Boo'?" Ratso cried.

I sighed. "Never mind. Just take my word for it. School is the wrong place for you to be. Believe me."

Just then I heard Mum coming. I had plenty of warning because she was into martial arts and used the stairs like a kind of mini-gym, going *"Ai-eee-ha!"* as she did knee-bends on every step.

Mum smiled as she came in and tickled the top of Ratso's head.

"He's so cute!" she said. "If I had my way the little darling would have the run of the house."

Ratso glared. "Tell your ma I am *not* cute!" he muttered. "I'm a teacher!"

"Oh, listen," cooed Mum. "It's almost as if he's trying to speak!"

Ratso glared even more.

"What was it you wanted, Mum?" I asked.

"Oh, yes," she said. "I've just been on the phone to Bobby's mum and she informs me there's a pet show at your school tomorrow. Why didn't you tell me?"

My heart sank to my trainers. I had hoped that Mum wouldn't hear about the show.

"Um – I forgot," I muttered.

Mum frowned. "Goodness me, Gary," she said. "You're so disorganized. It's a good job that I'm on the ball. So – about tomorrow – be sure you make little Ratso look all spick and span. He'll probably win the prize for cutest pet."

"But, Mum," I protested. "I can't take Ratso to school."

"Why ever not?" asked Mum, puzzled.

"He's… er… well, you see it's…" I shrugged hopelessly. For the life of me I couldn't think of one excuse.

"Oh, don't be silly!" said Mum. "I think you're just being lazy, that's all. Now, I want no arguments, Gary. You will take part in the pet show tomorrow with Ratso and that's final."

"But, Mum!" I wailed. "You don't understand."

"No arguments, Gary," Mum said and spun on her heel and stalked out.

"Great!" I moaned half-aloud and sank on to my bed. "Just great!" I glanced dejectedly at Ratso who was grinning from ear to ear. "I suppose you're happy now," I said.

"I sure am, pardner," Ratso said cheerily. "And you know – your ma ain't half-bad after all."

Chapter Two

"Boom… ba-ba boom… ta-raaaa!" The last dramatic chord of Tchaikovsky's 1812 Overture sounded in his earphones and Dad flung out his arms, nearly knocking Mum's cup of tea out of her hand.

"Tom!" she cried. "Be careful! You shouldn't be doing your conducting at breakfast."

Dad grinned sheepishly. "Sorry, Sue," he said. "But there's nothing like the 1812 for getting you going in the morning. All those wonderful explosions!"

"Why don't you take up martial arts, like me," replied Mum adjusting her karate head-band. "There's nothing like it for improving the circulation."

And with that, she jumped up, posed
dramatically and lashed out with one of
her feet – *"Hai-yaa!"* – knocking Dad's boiled
egg on to the floor.

"Looks like I'll just have to make do with
toast this morning," he sighed. Dad glanced at
Ratso sitting quietly in his cage and then back
to me as he began to butter another slice.

18

"I hear you're taking *thingy* to school this morning," he said slowly. "I was thinking I'd phone your Head Teacher and suggest that she keeps the rat permanently at the school. As a kind of – er – mascot."

I nearly choked on my egg.

"Wh–what?" I spluttered.

"I think it would be a good idea," Dad replied. "It would relieve you of the responsibility of looking after it. In fact, I think I'll phone right now."

He got up from the table.

"But, Dad," I protested, "you can't!"

I needn't have worried. Mum was outraged. "Tom!" she cried. "You'll do no such thing! Ratso is a part of our family now and he's going to stay!"

I breathed an inward sigh of relief and almost forgave Mum for insisting that I take Ratso to the pet show.

"Stop being so mean about the little thing,"
Mum went on as Dad sat down at the table
again. "He hasn't done you any harm."

Dad glowered. "I don't like the way it looks
at me," he muttered. "Feels like its tiny little
pink eyes are boring into my mind – trying to
find out what's inside."

J/11, 590

"That's exactly what I'm doing, mister," drawled Ratso quietly. "But I shouldn't worry – there's nothing much in there to get excited about."

I gave Ratso a look and the little alien grinned and winked.

Mum smiled as she came back to the table.

"Little Ratso's such a talker!" she said. "I wish I knew what he was saying."

Oh no you don't, Mum, I thought. Oh no you don't.

Chapter Three

On the way to school I met Bobby, my best friend. His pet was a stick insect called Bert and he had it in a box in his school bag. He knew Ratso's secret and had promised me he would never tell but I knew how much of a temptation it was for him to blab.

"What happened?" he asked. "I thought you said there was no way you were taking the alien to school."

"My mum happened," I muttered. "She insisted I take him so he could win the cutest pet title."

Bobby smirked. "I don't think so," he said. "Cute he is not." He peered at Ratso and the little alien chattered back at him.

"What did he say?" asked Bobby.

"He said thanks because he's fed up with being called cute."

"Don't mention it," said Bobby, grinning at Ratso. "In fact I'd go as far as to say you look positively ugly."

"Don't push it," I warned. "He might turn into a gorilla and beat you up."

Bobby grinned. "No chance," he said, then looked at Ratso warily. "On second thoughts," he muttered, "we *did* see him change into a monkey at the vet's."

"I'm not looking forward to this pet show," I sighed. "Not only will it be nerve-racking looking after Ratso but there's big Derek Butane as well. He's been making my life a misery at school."

"Yeah," agreed Bobby. "Big Butane – The Pain. He'll be swaggering about today with those two flea-bitten greyhounds that his dad races."

"Talk of the devil," I muttered as we reached the school gates and saw The Pain right ahead of us with his dogs. He was talking to his pals Jimmy and Kev and when he spotted me he let out a coarse laugh.

"Oi! Smith!" he yelled. "What's that you've got in the cage? A poxy little rat, is it? Haa! Keep it away from my dogs in case they think it's a rabbit! Ha-haa!"

"I wouldn't annoy the rat if I were you, Derek," said Bobby with a smug grin. "It might surprise you."

"Bobby!" I hissed and dug him in the ribs with my elbow. "Cut it out!"

"Yeah? We're all terrified," sneered The Pain. He reached out and swatted the cage. "Stupid little poxy pet!"

Ratso was furious.

"You no-good varmint! I ain't nobody's pet!" he yelled. "Quit shootin' off your big mouth. Nobody wants to hear your stupid talk no more. Get goin' before I bust out of this here jail and—"

"Shut up, Ratso," I hissed at him between gritted teeth and took off at a run towards the school entrance before the little alien became too excited and changed shape. I knew it looked as if I was running away but I couldn't help that. Behind me I heard The Pain laugh again.

"Ha-haa!" he roared. "Little Smithy's running away in case his poxy little rat gets eaten! Ha-haa!"

"I knew this was going to be a disaster," I muttered to myself. "I just knew it!"

Chapter Four

In the hall everything had been set up for the pet show. A day of the week had been allocated to each class so it was only the people in my class that were showing their pets today. I noticed that Gemma Price who lived next door to me had brought her two cats. The moggies had already tried to catch Ratso twice in my garden so I was pleased to see that the rodents' section and the cats' section were well apart.

As I walked into the hall my teacher, Mr Anderton, peered at Ratso and made a note on his clipboard.

"A rat is a rodent, Gary," he said and pointed with his pen. "It goes in the rodent section."

Mr Anderton must have done the same 'stating the obvious' course as Dad, I thought.

"Was that your teacher?" Ratso asked as I put his cage down.

I pretended to fiddle with the clasp on the door of his cage.

"Yes," I whispered. "But don't get any funny ideas about talking to him."

"Why not?" Ratso asked innocently. "He looks quite intelligent."

"Looks can be deceptive," I hissed. "And anyway, I told you before – he'd go ballistic! And you'd be putting yourself in danger."

"I ain't afraid of anything," Ratso replied staunchly.

"Please, Ratso," I said, "don't—"

"Talking to our poxy little pet, are we, Smithy?"

I jerked round and saw The Pain standing leering at me.

He pushed his big face close to mine.

"Whispering little love messages to it, were you, eh?"

He turned and called across the hall.

"Oi… Jimmy… Kev! Get this. Smithy's in love with his rat! Ha-haa!"

The Pain's friends started to laugh and Mr Anderton looked up from his clipboard.

"That's enough, Derek," he said mildly. "Go over and attend to your dogs."

"But Gary Smith's gone gaga, sir," said The Pain. "He loves a rat. He's going to marry it!"

More people heard him this time and a ripple of laughter ran round the hall.

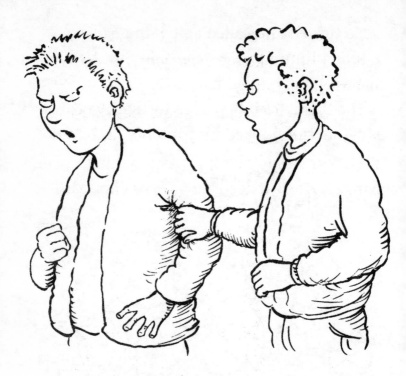

My blood boiled. I grabbed The Pain by the arm and spun him round to face me.

"Look," I ground out. "Cut it out! That's not funny!"

"Oh yeah?" sneered The Pain and pushed me away. "Says who?"

My heart was thumping as I pushed him back. "Says me," I said as forcefully as I could. "Just leave me alone."

The Pain grinned slowly.

"Or else you'll do what?" he snarled.

I gulped. A fist fight with The Pain after school now looked definitely on the cards – *not* my idea of fun.

"Or else—" I began, wondering what I was going to say next.

Luckily I didn't have to say anything. Mr Anderton arrived waving his clipboard.

"Stop it, you two," he snapped, "or you'll be doing detention after school."

He went up on to the stage to talk to Mr Atkins, the caretaker, and The Pain gave me an 'I'll get you later' look as he went over to his dogs.

"Not a good start to the day," Bobby observed. He started to chat about all the pets but I became aware that something was happening at the other end of the hall. There was a crowd round one of the tables and I could hear them chattering and laughing. Suddenly, out of all the hubbub, I heard one word distinctly. *Rat*. I felt myself go cold all over. Spinning round, I looked at Ratso's cage and my heart hit my trainers.

The door was open and Ratso was gone!

Chapter Five

"Ratso…" I gasped. "He's escaped!"

As Bobby gaped at the empty cage I dashed away and pushed into the crowd that was gathered round the table.

"Your rat thinks it's a teacher, Gary," Paula Weir chortled as I squeezed past. "It was writing on the board a moment ago and now it's reading the register. It's so funny!"

I got to the front of the crowd and nearly fainted. Ratso was on the teacher's table and really did have the class register open in front of him. There were strange marks on the board behind him which I took to be alien writing although they just looked like lines and squiggles. Then, with a horrible start I realized that Ratso really *was* reading from the register, calling out the names of the people in my class. He was attempting to pronounce the names in English but as I gazed around at my laughing classmates it slowly dawned on me that nobody could understand what Ratso was saying. He wasn't able to read anything out in English without sounding like a rat!

I saw him try to read the name Jonathon Brown but it came out sounding like "*Jo... wha... naee... squeak... pron... bar... owee... whee... en.*"

Then, to my horror, Bobby piped up excitedly as he too realized what Ratso was trying to do.

"He's talking to us!" he cried with a laugh. "Ratso's actually reading the register!" He turned to the others. Can't you hear him? He's a really smart rat. Did you know he's an—"

Desperately I pulled him aside. "No, Bobby," I hissed. "You promised!"

Bobby suddenly became aware of what he had done. "Oops! Sorry," he whispered. "Got carried away there."

I needn't have worried. Everybody thought it was all a big joke.

"Yeah! What a brilliant rat!" exclaimed Naz Patel with a grin. "It doesn't half make some funny noises."

Sam Lafferty snorted with laughter. "Just like Andy Pandy!"

Ratso suddenly gave up reading and began talking directly to me.

"Why in tarnation don't they understand me?" he stormed. "I thought I was reading your language pretty darn well!"

Fiona Pettigrew laughed out loud.

"Listen to him!" she cried. "Oh, Gary, your rat is so cute! When he makes those funny noises I could just cuddle him to bits!"

"Cute? Cute?!" raged Ratso hopping about in anger. "Is that all they think of me?" He looked around. "Where's your teacher? I'm sure he'll understand me."

Fiona giggled. "It really looks as if he's talking to you, Gary. Did you train him to do that?"

"Er – it's a kind of game," I said and edged along the table towards the irate little alien.

"Come on now, Ratso," I said, "let's get you
back in your cage."

Ratso backed away out of my reach.

"No way, pardner," he said. "I aim to do a bit
of teaching!"

He picked up the marker and began to write
on the board again.

The class roared with laughter.

"What's going on here?"

I turned and saw Mr Anderton pushing his
way through the crowd. Derek 'The Pain'
Butane was right behind him, grinning nastily.

It was obvious that he'd told the teacher what had happened. Mr Anderton blinked in annoyance when he saw Ratso.

"What is your rat doing to my nice clean board, Gary?" he cried. "Remove it immediately!"

"Oh, Mr Anderton," Sophie Miller pleaded. "Can't you leave Ratso there a bit longer? He's great!"

"And funny!" said Fiona Pettigrew.

The Pain gave her a nasty look and elbowed his way out of the crowd.

46

"I think Gary's rat is the coolest pet in this show, sir," Naz Patel piped up and lots of people said, "Yeah!"

Somebody began chanting "Ratso! Ratso!" and everybody joined in. "Ratso! Ratso! Ratso! Ratso!"

I made a move to grab Ratso but he nimbly jumped out of my reach.

"It's just like being back on *Whee*," he called to me above the noise. "I always was a very popular teacher, you know!"

"Gary!" Mr Anderton shouted angrily. "Pick up your pet – *now!*"

Before I could do anything, two furry shapes landed on the table. With a shock I recognized the next-door moggies. Somehow they had got loose!

The deadly duo sprang at Ratso but the little alien deftly jumped to the side. As the cats skidded past, however, one of them managed to knock Ratso over. He fell off the end of the table and Gemma Price's murderous moggies dived after him.

Everybody began screaming and shouting as the cats chased Ratso all over the hall. Picking up on the panic around them all the animals

and birds began to howl, bark, squeak and
twitter in alarm. Mr Anderton began giving
out orders to everyone to go and calm their
pets and he sent Gemma and me in pursuit of
the cats and Ratso.

I looked around desperately and saw that
the moggies had Ratso cornered at the back of
the stage. As I leapt on to it, Ratso jumped too
– on to a rickety shelf filled with broken table
tennis bats, plastic shuttlecocks, burst tennis
balls and old trainers. He dived behind the
pile of trainers and the cats followed him,
their paws scrabbling frantically for a
foothold. But the shelf wasn't strong enough.

In a noisy clatter of wood and plastic it crashed to the ground. The cats landed safely and shot away in panic. Gemma was right behind me and the moggies leapt into her arms.

I knelt down among the pile of debris.

"Ratso!" I hissed. "Where are you? It's all right now. You can come out." There was no reply. I searched all over the stage but Ratso had vanished. As I stood, baffled, scratching my head, I suddenly heard him calling to me.

"Pardner. Hey, pardner."

The voice was faint and seemed far away.

Then, with a start, I realized I was hearing it *inside my head!*

I whirled round, confused.

"I'm over here, pardner," Ratso said. "By the shoes."

I knelt down again and began moving the trainers aside gingerly. Some of them were very smelly.

"Where are you?" I whispered, holding my nose. "I can't see you."

"Ah! That's it, you've got me!" Ratso replied.

"What are you on about?" I hissed back. "*Please* don't say you're inside this smelly old trainer."

"*I'm* the smelly old trainer!" said Ratso testily. "I transformed myself to get away from those cannabalistic Earth pets."

I gaped at the trainer.

"Really?"

"Yup."

I whistled softly. "Brilliant." I glanced over my shoulder and saw that order had been restored in the hall and that Mr Anderton was walking purposefully towards me.

"Right, Ratso," I whispered urgently. "Change back. Now!"

"I'm afraid I can't do that right now, pardner," said the little alien's voice in my head. "You see, it usually takes a bit longer to change back to normal from being an object than it does from being an animal."

"How much longer?" I hissed anxiously.

"Oh, anything from a couple of minutes to a whole day," came the reply.

Chapter Six

"Have you found your pet rat yet, Gary?"

I turned. Mr Anderton was standing at the front of the stage with the glowering figure of Derek 'The Pain' Butane beside him.

I shook my head. "Not really, sir."

Mr Anderton nodded sympathetically.

"Don't worry. It'll turn up." He looked at The Pain and frowned. "It seems that Derek here was responsible for the upset a moment ago. He was spotted opening the cats' cage."

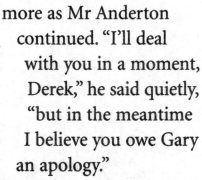

The Pain glowered even more as Mr Anderton continued. "I'll deal with you in a moment, Derek," he said quietly, "but in the meantime I believe you owe Gary an apology."

The hall became silent as everyone listened.

"Gary's waiting, Derek."

The Pain mumbled something and Mr Anderton shook his head.

"I beg your pardon?" he said. "Gary didn't catch that." He looked at me. "Did you, Gary?"

I shook my head. "No, sir," I said.

Mr Anderton turned back to The Pain.

"Louder, please," he said.

"Sorry," Derek muttered, scowling.

"Not good enough," snapped Mr Anderton. "Say it like you mean it, boy! Loudly!"

This time everyone in the hall heard it.

"Sorry, Gary," said Derek Butane.

I felt my insides give a happy little jump and at the same time heard Bobby and some of my friends say "Yes!"

But The Pain threw me a nasty look and I knew that I'd have to face him sooner or later.

"I'm sure your rat will turn up soon, Gary," said Mr Anderton as he turned away with The Pain. "In the meantime come down here and help with the show." He pointed at the trainer in my hand. "Put that back on the pile. Mr Atkins is going to give them to the recycling centre to be mashed up."

"What?" I gasped. "I mean – er – couldn't I just look a bit longer, sir?" I pleaded. "Ratso might be hiding here somewhere."

"Well, all right," replied Mr Anderton. "But don't be long."

I stared at the smelly trainer. What am I going to do? I thought.

Ratso answered me telepathically.

"Hide me somewhere, pardner. So's when I change back nobody will notice."

"Good idea," I muttered and looked around for a hiding place. Just as I spotted one, the trainer was suddenly whisked from my hands by Mr Atkins.

"Thanks," he said, grinning. "This stuff's all going out, lad." And he popped the shoe into a black plastic bag and began to throw the other debris on top of it. "The lorry from the recycling centre comes this morning. Just in time for this lot."

I found my voice at last.

"But, Mr Atkins," I cried in horror, "you can't throw that lot out!"

The caretaker looked at me curiously.

"Why not, lad?"

"My pet rat, Mr Atkins," I went on desperately. "It's missing and it might be in your bag."

"Eh?" Mr Atkins shook his head. "Don't be daft, lad. I put all this stuff in here myself, and there was no rat!"

"But it might be hiding in one of the trainers," I said anxiously.

Mr Atkins shook his head again and swung the bag over his shoulder.

"Don't be daft," he repeated. "No self-respecting pet would hide in one of those smelly objects."

I heard all the stuff knock together as he walked away.

"Tarnation! That hurt! Ow!"

It was Ratso. And this time his voice wasn't in my head. I heard it with my ears. He had changed back!

I rushed after Mr Atkins and grabbed the bag from him.

"Hey!" he cried. "What are you up to?!"

"I'm sorry, Mr Atkins," I said as I quickly opened the bag. "But my rat really *is* in here."

I thrust my hands in among the trainers and, to the amazement of the caretaker, lifted out a white rat.

Ratso sneezed.

"Phew!" he said. "I'm sure glad not to be smelly any more!" He stretched his arms. "That's a relief. I was getting really stiff being a shoe." He looked at me and sighed. "And you were right after all, pardner," he said. "Your school is definitely the wrong place to be."

The little alien looked so crestfallen that I asked permission to take Ratso back home. Mr Anderton was just delighted that everything had turned out well in the end and he agreed right away.

When I got back to school I found that everyone in my class, with the notable exception of The Pain, had been so impressed with Ratso that they had got together and made him a little certificate.

It said:

Unofficial Pet Show Award

COOLEST PET IN SCHOOL

— RATSO —

(A funnier teacher than Mr Anderton)

When I showed it to Mum that evening she was delighted.

"I knew it!" she cried, tickling the top of Ratso's head. "Cuteness like Ratso's could never go unrecognized!"

Dad groaned and went off to the cassette player in the kitchen to conduct the noisiest bit of music he could find.

I took Ratso upstairs to my room.

"Well," I said. "What did you think of my school, then?"

"Dangerous," he said.

"I tend to agree with you," I replied. "The Pain's been warned off for now but he'll be after me again as soon as the fuss has died down." I sighed. "School is certainly not going to be dull for me in the next few weeks, I can tell you."

Ratso grinned. "Yeah. It was scary… but I kinda liked it," he said. "So, when can I go back?"

"You don't mean it!" I gasped.

"I surely do, pardner," replied the little alien. "I surely do!"

Oh no, I thought. Here we go again!

My Rat is ...

By Frank Rodgers

An exciting new Mega Stars series

Gary's rat is no ordinary pet.
Ratso is an alien from another planet.
An alien who's crash-landed in Gary's back garden...

Catch up with Ratso in these other stories:

My Rat is an Alien

Will Ratso be eaten by the local
moggies? And can Gary stop
anyone finding out about him?

My Rat is a Hero

Ratso stows away on a school trip to
the seaside, and Gary is furious...
at first. But when there's trouble,
Ratso saves the day...

My Rat is a Cowboy

Ratso crash lands his spaceship on
a pony farm. Now he can be a *real*
cowboy. But one alien rat can cause
havoc on a horse...

For more information about Mega Stars, please contact:
The Sales Department, Macdonald Young Books,
61 Western Road, Hove, East Sussex BN3 1JD